ONE-OH-EIGHT

Anne Stobbs

John and Adele Miller
from Anne Stobbs
(not Miller!)

Published by Bucks Literary Services, Marsworth, Bucks

Bucks Literary Services,
Marsworth, Bucks

ONE-OH-EIGHT MILLER: *First published 1989*

ISBN 0-9515518-0-9
One-Oh-Eight Miller.

Illustrations and cover by Frankie Warren

Set in 12pt New Century Schoolbook by
Keyword, Tring, Herts.

Printed and bound by Copeland Sales, Berkhamsted, Herts.

British Library Cataloguing
Publication Data
Stobbs, Anne 1922 —
One Oh Eight Miller
1. Great Britain Royal Airforce
Women's Auxiliary Airforce Biographies
I. Title 358.41348092

Thank You

To my daughter Frankie Warren for the illustrations and cover for this book.

To my daughter Mandy for the loan of her word processor and endless patience with my struggles with it.

To my daughter Louisa for her advice with marketing.

And

To the Waafs I served with.

Bless 'em All!

INTRODUCTION

You never forget your service number. I'll bet anybody that if you went up to fifty people at random who ever served in the Forces they would rattle off their service number without even pausing to scratch their heads.

When they paid you in the war, weekly, they lined you all up (standing at ease) and called out your "last three" and surname. Week after week I'd stand there, dozing through the alphabet, until suddenly it was "ONE OH EIGHT MILLER!!" and my turn at last to march up to the table and receive a carefully counted pile of coins amounting to about thirty bob (£1.50), salute smartly, and march back to my place.

That's why I've called this book "One-oh-eight Miller", because it's just the story of a very ordinary Waaf; one of thousands, with nothing heroic or important happening to her. But it might interest and perhaps amuse those readers who were not there and revive some memories for those who were and bring a reminiscent smile to their faces.

1. JOINING UP

My father, of course, wanted me to go into the Army. He was a regular Gunner and he actually rejoined his regiment on 3rd September 1939 (a source of great satisfaction to him!).

But I told him that I'd be damned if I'd spend the war dressed in that unbecoming khaki, so, to his disgust, I chose the RAF purely on the strength of the prettier blue uniform!

And so it came about that in the depths of the rather unpleasant, cold, wet winter of 1943, I presented myself at the recruiting depot in Chatham very early one morning, and met the small contingent of girls who were joining up with me. We were to make our way to Innsworth in Gloucestershire, to what was known as the Induction Centre.

The recruiting officer at Chatham decided that he would put me in charge of transporting this little lot to its destination. I wondered why he did this, but by the time we arrived at Paddington Station, I guessed why. It turned out that none of the others had ever been through London before. They lived so near it, but they were like foreigners there. I remember descending into the underground with them, and realising that they were all terrified. They were terrified of the escalator, terrified of the electric rails, terrified of the train itself. I had to ride up and down the escalator half a dozen times to demonstrate how safe it was before any of them would set foot on it, and at one moment I was really scared that they would all run away in a blind panic; that I'd never get them across London and I'd be blamed for everything. I was barely twenty, and had never been put in charge of anything more serious than a lacrosse team before in my life.

Somehow we all arrived at Paddington in one piece, and met some 300 others, all heading for Innsworth.

Train journeys during the war were something of an adventure in themselves. No train ever ran on time; they were liable to be several hours late. They seldom went by the direct route, but were prone to wander off more or less aimlessly up little branch lines (long since Beechinged) and to halt for hours in the midst of nowhere. They were always crammed to capacity; you usually sat on the floor in the corridor or on kitbags or luggage; they never had any heating working and often no lighting; what little lighting they did have was a dim blue, for the blackout. The reason for their diversions was usually the passage of munitions or troop trains, which always had top priority, and all other trains were shunted aside to give them fast and uninterrupted journeys. Perfectly sensible, really, but perfectly damnable for everyone else.

Our arrival at Innsworth is etched deeply into my memory. I doubt if any woman who ever arrived there will have forgotten it. I suppose I was lucky in a way; I'd been at a boarding school and was therefore unlikely to suffer from homesickness, and used to living in dormitories. But no girls' dormitory was ever like this! And neither had my fellow boarders given me any preparation for the sights that were to greet me on my first experience of an F.F.I!

None of us knew what an F.F.I was and nobody saw fit to enlighten us. We were merely told to get undressed right down to our knickers and wrap a bath towel (small) around our shoulders. We were then herded into a very long line indeed, to await our turn for examination by the doctors.

FREE FROM INFECTION. That's what FFI stood for. A rather degrading little search for the telltale signs of all sorts of unpleasant things which the Royal Air Force felt they would prefer us to be free from.

I stood there in this long line and tried hard not to stare. It was rude to stare. But – heavens above – was it possible that the human female anatomy could come in such incredible shapes and sizes? I simply couldn't believe it. I suppose in those days there wasn't so much fuss about slimming, and even quite young girls could be extraordinarily bulgy! Older ones could be even bulgier.

I stood marvelling, and shuddering a bit, until at last I reached the front, and submitted to a request to perform what might be described as a quick flash (knickers down) for the benefit of the doctor. He looked carefully at everything he saw, made us turn round slowly in front of him, looked at our teeth, and passed us over to a ferocious-looking female NCO who proceeded to go through our hair with a fine (very fine) toothcomb.

And it was at this stage that I lost every single one of my companions from Chatham. Not one of them passed the hair examination! In fact it was the last I ever saw of them. I wonder what fate befell them all...

But most of us were finally allowed to dress again, and were shown to our sleeping huts, 35 to a hut. The beds had straw palliasses, four blankets, and a pillow so flabby we stuffed clothing into it to make it more comfortable! It must have been around midnight when we finally fell into an exhausted sleep and my early start from Chatham seemed light years away.

Incidentally this really primitive bed seems to have been exclusive to Innsworth, probably with the idea of jolting all the civilians into reality and alerting them to the sort of thing that lay ahead. But on subsequent stations the bedding was a slight improvement on this, though only slight. Most service people slept on "biscuits". These consisted of a mattress divided, like all Gaul, in three parts. These were stuffed with hair or flock or something, and buttoned, and were a pale fawn colour, and so they were called biscuits because they did rather resemble a dog biscuit (and they felt a bit like them too when you lay down.) The reason for slicing them into three sections was so that when you made your bed in the morning, you could stack them all up, one on top of the other, with folded blankets on top of them, sheets on top of them, and pillow on top of all that. (Girls had sheets; men didn't).

Now please don't ask me whose idea it was to have this bed stacking done every morning, or who thought that beds look smarter that way, with all their springs showing. But the fiendish plot which lay behind it all was that the officer, when inspecting a barrack hut, could observe through the bedsprings whether the floor was filthy or not.

Anyway, with an extremely small sheet to hold them together, it was inevitable that the three sections came apart in the night, and you would wake to find yourself lying on the bare springs between the biscuits, or quite often with one biscuit entirely missing, fallen on the floor.

But I digress. Back to our first day at Innsworth, which dawned with a 6 o'clock bugle call on the tannoy, and first thing after breakfast we had our photographs taken (for passes) and then had to hand in our civilian ration books, identity cards and clothing coupons.

We were civilians no longer...

Next came our uniform. We all queued up again, this time in a huge hangar, and were handed, first a kitbag, and then item after item of clothing and equipment. I was terribly impressed with the trouble they took to make us look as smart as possible, even to the lengths of having a tailor on duty to do quick alterations where needed. I wrote home that "the quality of the clothing is quite marvellous. If you have battledress you are issued with Woolsey woollen socks; the shoes are made of leather you'd pay 45 shillings for in peacetime – lovely soft, pliable stuff such as you can't buy anywhere nowadays. The undies, too, are of very good quality. Our winter knickers (pale blue wool) are known as 'twilights' and the summer ones (dark blue cotton) are 'blackouts'!"

We worked our way slowly along the trestle tables being handed tunic, skirt, cap, capbadge, greatcoat, item after item, all of which were stuffed into the kitbag.

I never understood why servicewomen were given kitbags. Hardly any of us could hoist them successfully on to our shoulders the way the men did. So we inevitably dragged them for miles along the ground, making holes in the bottom through which odd socks dropped, or bras, never to be seen again. And this led you into dire trouble, as we were soon to find out, when we had our first kit inspection that day.

This was the beginning of what quickly became a nightmare in my life. Regularly for the rest of my career in His Majesty's Forces, I was required to lay out all this paraphernalia all over my bed, in a certain prescribed pattern, for it to be inspected and the inevitable missing items noticed, with terrifying repercussions. You could be put on a charge for losing something. You could be required to pay for a new one out of your own pocket, which was always empty. Nothing belonged to you; it belonged to the King. I can't recall ever having everything I should have had on any kit inspection I ever endured (except that first one) and I came to dread and loathe them with all my heart.

Anyway that first one went off fine (even I could hardly lose anything so quickly as that) and the rest of the day was spent mostly sewing on all the badges (with the aid of a sewing kit known as a 'huzzif' we'd been issued with.)

Then we were taught about cleaning buttons and cap badges. Altogether there were eight buttons on your tunic and ten on your greatcoat, a buckle and a cap badge to polish. We were issued with a button stick, which enables you to scoop four or five buttons together and clean them all at once without getting polish on the material. We used mostly the impregnated cotton wool type of polish, though some painfully keen types used to buy Silvo out of their own pocket, to try and outshine everybody else. It was forbidden to cover your buttons with amylacetate to avoid having to polish them. Lots of people tried it on, but a hawk-eyed officer inspecting a parade could spot it easily and there'd be hell to pay. We used to envy the Navy, who have buttons of a special metal to resist the salt air, and which don't have to be polished at all.

However, a certain amount of pride insinuated itself into this spit and polish business, and people who had been in the service a long time, if they polished away like mad several times a week, could eventually achieve a state where the insignia on buttons and the detail on cap badge were almost entirely obliterated. In other words, you'd have quite a job to see that they were in the RAF at all! This was considered a highly desirable status to have reached, and much envied by us raw recruits whose brasswork was a nasty yellowy colour and very deeply etched.

They taught us also how to look after the huts we lived in. Nearly all the huts I ever lived in were Nissens, as were also the radar ops huts.

There is something about a Nissen hut which has an indefinable but very definite effect on the people who inhabit it. I don't know who Mr Nissen was, and I'm sure his idea for knocking up cheap accommodation for masses of human beings was an admirable one, but the fact remains that it's very like living inside a barrel, and it gets you down in time. They were made of corrugated iron, with brick ends to them, and although I dare say your average, run-of-the-mill chicken wouldn't mind being cooped up in one, I think most of the human beings who had to spend so many years in them began to feel a curious type of corrugated claustrophobia creeping over them.

The floors of these jolly dwellings were covered in brown lino. Very nasty. A piece of the floor with an invisible demarcation line around it was known as your "bed space" and for this you were entirely responsible, plus a share of the communal area in the middle. Every hut had a big iron stove in the middle, with a big iron pipe to let the smoke out through the roof. A great deal of one's life took place around this fire in winter time, sitting on hard little chairs, scorching the soles of your shoes on the hot metal, and gossiping by the hour.

The floors were always polished with sanitary towels. Each hut was issued with one of those awful heavy, swinging polisher things, and an S.T would be fastened to this by means of its loops, liquid polish would be splashed around, and away you'd go.

The S.Ts came courtesy of Lord Nuffield. I don't suppose he knew this fact, but he had made a donation of a million pounds or so to the women's services and they decided to use it to provide us with free S.Ts. Though I doubt if they intended us to use them to polish the lino with!

One last operation was necessary before we could leave Innsworth and proceed to our square-bashing training.

One of the privileges which volunteers enjoyed over conscripts was that you were allowed to choose your "trade" as it was called. (Within the limits, that is, of those trades which happened to be available at the time you joined up).

Another privilege, incidentally, was that if you were thoroughly miserable, you were allowed, within a certain time of joining, to discharge yourself and go home again (there to await your call-up papers, when you would have to start all over again, and even go through Innsworth again, so it was scarcely worth the trouble).

I believe there was another kind of "privilege" associated with having a baby (by mistake). If you'd joined up, you could stay at home to look after it; but if you were a conscript you had to go home, have your baby and return again within a matter of months.

Well, when it came my turn for the trade testing and interviewing, I had decided that I'd had enough of office life and so would keep mum about my secretarial training and try something new. The trade-testing sergeant asked me what I'd like to do.

I'd often seen glimpses in films of some very important-looking Waafs who seemed to be pushing things around with croupier's rakes on a huge table with a map on it. I told him that I rather fancied being one of those.

"Ah, that's a Radar Operator", he said. "You with your School Certificate would do all right there." I was given a test which I passed, so down went my name with Radar Operator beside it, and that was how I came to spend the rest of the war staring into a cathode ray tube! The people who shoved things around with croupier's rakes were plotters of course, and their job in fact was to indicate on a huge map the whereabouts of bomber and fighter groups so that the senior officers in charge of the battle could see at a glance how things were progressing. In fact the movements they made were dictated by the information passed to them on an intercom *by* the radar operators, who were getting this information from what they saw on their cathode ray tubes.

Such are the dictates of fate!

Would I have been happier as a plotter? Who knows?

At least my trade allowed me to sit down most of the time, which is more than theirs did, and of course we considered our trade to be vastly superior to theirs; but then people on radar considered themselves superior to almost everyone, except possibly pilots. And even them only by a whisker.

But it's funny to think that the sole and only reason why I did what I did in the war was because the chap in charge of allocating trades didn't know one trade from another!

In the short time we remained at Innsworth we were trying hard to get used to wearing a uniform and it did take quite a bit of getting used to. It was, of course, thoroughly unfeminine, with a collar and tie, the collar, separate with studs, and "trubenised" which meant it was stiff and sawed into your neck; a tunic with two upper pockets and two lower ones, into which you had to stuff everything which had previously gone into your handbag, thus ensuring that you bulged everywhere. Later on, they provided service women with a regulation shoulder bag, which made life a lot easier. But you just try wearing a straight skirt with no pocket, a short, belted tunic on top of that, and stowing away in its four pockets a handkerchief, comb, makeup, money and paybook, without looking a very funny shape indeed.

Then there was the business of our hair, which was a perpetual bugbear. It had to be off the collar. Now if you wear a shirt with trubenised collar and your hair must be off that collar, your hair is going to be very short indeed. The fashion of the day was for long hair down to your shoulders, as you can see from any film of the 40s (and we all wanted to look exactly like Ginger Rogers or Dorothy Lamour.) So the only thing to do was to devise a method of getting rid of your hair when you were in uniform, but still being able to let it down when you got into evening dress to go to dances on leave. (Dances in camp were strictly in uniform.)

In the end what most of us did was to twist an old, laddered silk stocking and tie it round our heads, then roll all our hair ends up and tuck them into it, making it look like a big fat sausage. Then, when you wanted to look glamorous, off came the stocking and down came your hair. Magic!

Makeup was restricted to the bearest minimum, though a lot of girls ignored this rule. We usually wore lisle stockings with our uniform (lisle is now defunct I think, thank goodness.) But you were allowed to wear silk at a dance (grey, as were the lisle).

And so, with the trades all selected and the uniforms all provided and the hair duly off the collar, we all loaded up our kitbags and set off for Morecambe in Lancashire for our "square-bashing" training.

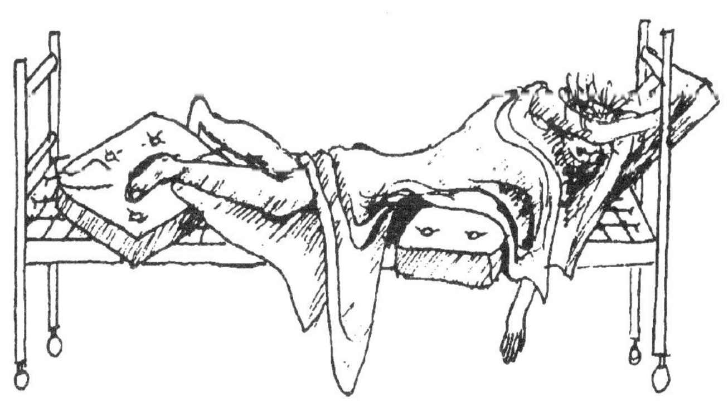

2. SQUARE BASHING

Morecambe didn't look much like it does today. The sea was almost invisible behind its barricade of barbed wire and tank traps. I suppose we did like to be beside the seaside (even in January) and to walk along the prom-prom-prom, though the only band which went tiddly-om-pom-pom was our own RAF band when we finally "passed out" at the end of the three weeks.

We didn't exactly bash the square, because there wasn't one, so we bashed the prom instead. Every day we were out there, usually in the pouring rain, wearing an amazing garment known as a ground sheet/cape (a huge rubber tent which fastened at the neck); and every day we were shouted at and screamed at and insulted and bullied and wheedled and cajoled into turning ourselves into a well-drilled, quite commendably smart body of women, instead of a collection of individuals which we were when we arrived.

I expect most people nowadays have seen service women marching and know how very well they can do it. We really did become quite proud of ourselves after a while, and acquired a certain satisfaction – even exhilaration – in becoming part of a squad which had learned to move as one, to turn, march, wheel, salute, eyes left, eyes right, and to do these things in unison, keeping dead straight lines, knowing that you're looking rather good.

Even the actual bashing of the square can be quite fun: ATTEN...SHUN! STANDAT...ICE! and all the shoes come crashing down at the same moment and make a lovely satisfying BANG!!

We were drilled by men but we were also drilled by women, and believe me, some of the women were even more frightening than the men. I can see one of them now – a great big sturdy blonde sergeant: *"Ef, roi', Ef, roi', Ef, roi' – you got two left feet?"* she'd bawl at us, and if you laughed she'd bawl something worse.

We didn't bash the prom all day long though. In between times, we were marched around from cinema to cinema all over Morecambe; no, not to see a movie, no such luck. They were used as lecture halls and it was here that we were indoctrinated into some of the many rules and regulations and customs we ought to know about.

"Ignorance of the Rules is unacceptable as an excuse," they said, and I soon found this to be true when I went home for my first ever 48 hour pass. My train back missed its connection at Euston (as usual) and I was late returning to camp (after 2359 hours, that magic witching hour when passes expired.)

I should have reported to a person called the RTO at Euston (Railway Transport Officer) who would have endorsed my pass and confirmed that I was late back through no fault of my own. I had not done so, having panicked and forgotten all the rules, and was duly placed on a Two-Five-Two.

Horror of all horrors – a charge so early in my career. "Caps orf! Ef, roi', ef, roi'," in front of the Admin Officer and three days confined to camp.

This turned out to be worse than it sounded. I didn't mind being confined to camp at all, but I did mind when I found myself down on hands and knees scrubbing literally acres of stone kitchen floors! (Stone or concrete, I forget.) This was known as "jankers" and they always found something particularly horrible for you to occupy your time with. Scrubbing potatoes would have been a doddle compared with those terrible floors. I think my knees were permanently injured during those three days.

From Morecambe I wrote the following in a letter home:

"Last Thursday we had a 3-mile long run along the front (I came in 19th out of about 400 and got a point for my squadron!) Immediately following this, without a moment's pause, we had *country dancing*!!

"Next day we paraded at 2.30 with our gas equipment, greatcoat on, haversack, gas mask and cape rolled up on top, with our ground sheets over all that (as needless to say it was pelting cats and dogs.) As the afternoon wore on and there was no chance of sitting down, just endless marching through the rain with a driving east wind, we began to feel more than a little weary. So we finished up with a rehearsal for our passing out parade!

"Then came Saturday, with the passing out parade, which was terrific with our own band. Immediately after that we had our second innoculation, which made us feel terribly ill, running temperatures. We couldn't raise or lower our left arms and had to help each other undress, eat our food on a fork, do each other's hair and almost wash each other!

"Next day we paraded again in pouring rain as usual and marched until we were soaked right through to the bones, whereupon we were delivered at a cinema (shoes, stockings completely waterlogged), sat down and given a gramophone recital for an hour and a half! L'Apres Midi d'un faun, Beethoven's violin concerto with Kreisler, etc etc!"

I can still clearly remember this concert incident! I suppose the RAF thought we'd better have our ration of culture for the good of our souls. And very nice too, if only we'd been nice and dry at the time!

Memories of Morecambe are almost entirely of rain and hypodermic needles! We were injected almost daily – TAB, tetanus, typhoid, diphtheria – you name it we got it, and nearly always in the cookhouse (which is not the place where you cook, but the place where you eat.)

I can see us all now, standing in long queues (as usual), waiting for our moment to come, with the men down one side of the room and the women down the other, and the men keeling over in a dead faint at about twice the rate of the women, usually before they ever got within sight of the needle!

But we learned a lot at Morecambe, and by the time we had that passing out parade, we felt we were fully-fledged Waafs and ready to go on to the next stage, which was training to learn your trade.

In my case this was to take me to Yatesbury in Wiltshire and details of the journey down there from Morecambe were described in a letter home dated 6 February 1943:

"We got up at 3.30 am and had breakfast at 4,

proceeded to the Naafi in the pitch dark, pouring with rain, with our respirators, tin hats, gas capes, ground sheets, and two ration bags strapped on various parts of our anatomy. We were then marshalled, proceeded to the station, collected our kit bags, slung them onto our already overburdened shoulders, and entrained. The train then proceeded to remain perfectly stationery for an hour and a half, what time we endeavoured to catch up with lost sleep.

"At 7.15 we steamed out of Morecambe with loud cheers, and then settled down for more sleep. We changed at a place called Pontypool Road, or rather we piled out while they slipped a couple of coaches and then we all piled back into the same ruddy train again (this is known as Air Force manoevres.)

"We then proceeded to Bristol where we changed again, this time into a different train. We had got the whole of this way without so much as a drop of water, let alone a nice hot cupper tea. We had been chewing on leathery sandwiches and pieces of wet pudding resembling bath loofah soaked in washing-up water, for a period of 13 hours.

"At 6.15 am we arrived at Calne as the dawn was breaking. We bundled out and dragged our kitbags half a mile to where transport was to meet us. Transport didn't meet us, or at least it did after we'd stood out in the cold for three-quarters of an hour, and when it arrived it consisted of one medium-sized lorry, into which two RAF chaps proceeded to throw, first our kitbags and then us – 26 of each, and there I lay, half on the ledge round the side of the lorry, with three kitbags, a suitcase and an RAF corporal on top of me, and the edge of someone's tin hat driving itself into my thigh.

"We travelled thus some five miles, and then reached the station; crawled out and reported at the Guard House, then proceeded back into the lorry again! One girl by this time was in a dead faint and the rest of us wished we were!

"The lorry stopped again and once more we tumbled out of it and stood shivering while our kitbags were distributed to us. We then dragged all our clobber half a mile or so to our hut.

"Next day we had eye tests, lectures all afternoon, and then – can you believe this – we were put straight on the 6 to midnight watch! And I mean real duty, in a real radar ops room!!"

I re-read this letter now and I find it all very hard to believe, yet it was entirely true as I wrote it at the time and I have the letter in front of me now. We had got up at 3.30 am for that journey, and finally arrived the following morning at 6.15 am and were put on the evening watch the very next day!

And so we began to realise that life in the Forces was not going to be a "piece of cake". Not at all... Life was real. Life was earnest!

3. YATESBURY

Yatesbury – a tiny place near Calne, set in the rolling open spaces of Wiltshire – was where they had chosen to teach us about Radar.

Radar, as most people know, was one of our success stories of the war. Dear old England actually gave birth to radar (through the brilliance of Sir Robert Watson Watt) and what's more, not only in the right place, but at the right time. Nobody could possible have come up with a more propitious invention at that moment in history, and to all intents and purposes I believe it won the war for us. I know that The Few won the Battle of Britain, but how would they have managed if they'd had no idea where in the whole sky to find the enemy?

There were several different kinds of radar, which were evolving all the time the war progressed; but they divided roughly into two main kinds: defensive and offensive. Defensive radar was in the business of scanning the sky for the enemy, plotting their movements, and seeing that they were engaged by our defences. Offensive radar was all about navigation, and was used by our own bombers, and also by the Royal Navy.

There were three main kinds of defensive radar in 1943: C.H. which stood for Chain Home; C.H.L. which was Chain Home Lowflying; and G.C.I./A.I. which stood for Ground Control Interception/Air Interception, which was a very clever idea whereby the enemy was spotted by the ground radar first and then transferred to the radar screen in a Mosquito or Beaufighter, which could then home in on him without further assistance from the ground.

The radar which I was to be trained on was C.H. These chains had actually been set up four months before war was declared. Very roughly speaking, there was a transmitter sending out signals and a receiver picking up the "echoes" which came back after the radio waves hit a force of bombers. These echoes appeared on a cathode ray tube (such as you have in a television set), and since we know the speed of radio waves, you need only to calibrate your cathode ray tube to measure the time that the wave has taken to reach you from the target, and therefore to know how far away they are and in which direction.

By other cunning means it was possible to work out, a little less accurately, the height.

The radar team were therefore supposed to (a) pick up the echo; (b) D-F it, which meant direction-find; (c) convert the information they received into a "plot" and then (d) relay this information by R.T. to the people with the croupier's rakes. ("Charlie Oboe Nin-er fife two!")

We worked in little teams, and once you got the hang of it, it wasn't difficult and was very rewarding, because you could, in effect, actually *see* those Jerry bombers gathering over France and heading towards you across the Channel, and, better still, *do* something about them.

It was exciting when you'd been reporting a bomber formation building up on the other side of the Channel and watching its approach towards England to observe suddenly the beginnings of a few little immature echoes gradually converge until they mingled into one enormous group, and then you knew there was a dogfight on. There were even occasions when you plotted the incoming bombers on your screen for half an hour or so, and eventually realised they were coming straight towards you, and then you could nip outside and finish off your reporting with a "visual". Then there were the other occasions when the echoes turned out to be a flock of migrating geese!

There was an extra little device – very clever – to enable you to distinguish the enemy echoes from those of our own planes. I.F.F. it was called: Identification Friend or Foe. This enabled us to "question" a plane and receive a signal consisting of a sort of downward blipping, indicating that it was Friend.

At Yatesbury we knew nothing of all this when we arrived of course. Radar was a desperately secret trade and we all took a secrecy oath which to the best of my knowledge was kept absolutely faithfully throughout the war. They say that women can't keep a secret, but it really isn't true!

Our course was six weeks, and it was amazing how much information they crammed into us in the time. Most of us knew nothing at all about radio and here the male operators-to-be had the advantage over us, since a lot of them knew a good deal about radio and had, in some cases, been working in radio shops before they joined up.

Those who had experience in radio usually became

radar mechanics rather than operators. They were the clever people who maintained and serviced all the complicated and sophisticated apparatus. Ex-telephone engineers were also invaluable in this trade; not only did transmitters and receivers have to be kept in perfect working order 24 hours a day, but also the land lines which linked them all to each other and to the plotting stations by intercom. There was an enormous amount of intricate machinery to be looked after, and most beautifully looked after it was.

(Of course, if a chap had been a qualified post office engineer and had encountered *my* recruiting sergeant, he'd probably have finished up by becoming a cook, or a clerk. But some of them must have been better at recruiting because there were certainly a lot of square pegs in square holes in the RAF.)

As for me, my mathematical education had finished at the square on the side of the hypotenuse, and I'd always found the subject difficult (which of course was why my recruiting chap had decided I was just right for Radar! But of course we *had* both thought I was going to be a plotter ...)

So I found the training very difficult, although the tuition must have been clever since I can, to this day, give a very sketchy explanation of how a cathode ray tube works, and I can tell you the speed of radio waves and light, and can recall quite a few odd scraps of information about what sine waves and carrier waves and things like that are. Which is not bad, considering that all this happened over forty years ago and I've never given the subject a moment's thought since then!

It was, in fact, not necessary to know very much about the science of radar in order to operate it, and I wonder they thought it necessary to teach us so much about it. I still pay tribute to their teaching, though, because in me they had pretty stony ground to sow the seed, and yet some of it took root and stayed for ever.

Alas, I was only about half way through the course when I suddenly got mumps! Of all the moments to fall sick! It couldn't have been worse for me, because I was promptly driven off in an ambulance to the RAF Hospital at Wroughton near Swindon, where I languished for two weeks or so until I was not infectious any longer; by which time my course had finished and all my friends been posted off to pastures new. I wasn't even allowed to start again at the beginning of the course, but had to join at the point I'd reached when I went sick. Very cruel this; I could remember nothing, and had an awful job to keep up.

I did have rather fun in the hospital, however. There was only one other person there with mumps, a most attractive Canadian pilot, and once we both ceased to feel like death, we were allowed and in fact encouraged to visit each other in order to keep ourselves occupied. This we succeeded in doing with no trouble at all. We started cautiously with games of draughts and finished up getting rather more enthusiastic about each other than the nurses would probably have thought good for us. We used to keep the draughts board carefully arranged ready to change games hastily when we heard one of them coming.

He was a delightful chap, my friend "Mumpy" and I felt thoroughly gloomy when the day came for him to be discharged fit and I had to remain a few more days with no one to talk to except, from a distance, a small contingent of unfortunate men who'd been given a funny batch of yellow fever vaccine in readiness for a far east posting, and who'd all contracted jaundice. They didn't look very attractive, poor things, all yellow; no substitute for my Canadian who'd looked a lot better even with his face all swollen up.

Ships that pass in the night, I thought sadly, as I waved him off. Wartime was full of them. But a year or so later, I was with some friends one evening in the Captain's Cabin in London when I suddenly heard a great shout across the bar: "HI THERE MUMPY!" and I turned round to find my Canadian standing there with a huge grin on his face. When we'd finally stopped hugging each other, we introduced our friends and a *very* riotous evening took off, which finally ended at heaven knows what small hour of the morning, in heaven knows which night club.

Anyway I had to catch up on the course somehow or other, and at last it was over and we were all posted off to various stations, with our brand new "sparks" badges sewn on our sleeves to show we were proper radar operators.

My family could never understand why I didn't try and get a commission. There were several reasons for this, one being that I really joined up too late. They had about all the officers they needed by then. And in the field of radar, officers were highly qualified people, usually with physics degrees. You could have a go at being at Admin. Officer, but few people on radar would have wanted to be one of these. They were never very popular with us: I think partly because they found themselves in rather a difficult position on a radar station.

All personnel were divided into "tech" and "non-tech"

and the non-techs, which included the Admin. Officer, were not allowed to set foot inside the Ops. Room, nor did they have the faintest idea what we were all doing in there! It must have been a tiresome situation for them and I think it soured their outlook towards us girls a bit. No wonder I never fancied being one of them myself, and I never heard of any girl on radar who did. I'll tell you a story, later on, about one of them; perhaps an extreme example but astonishingly a true one ...

4. MY FIRST RADAR CAMP

When I was told that I'd been posted to Dunkirk, I got a bit of a fright, because I thought that most of His Majesty's forces had managed to escape from that place, and it didn't seem fair to send me off there all on my own. But of course it wasn't the French Dunkirk, but the English one, near Canterbury in Kent.

It was in many ways a lovely place to be sent, even in 1943. In the heart of the Kentish countryside, close to Faversham and Canterbury and Whitstable, so that there were nice places to go to on "liberty runs" and plenty of cinemas, hostelleries etc to spend your off-time in. Not to mention London within easy reach. Compared with one or two stations I later found myself on, this was a pretty cushy one.

Of course it wouldn't have been, a little earlier on. It was one of the front-line radar stations in the Battle of Britain and they had played a big part in those memorable months. Anyone who can say they were at Dunkirk in the summer of 1940 can say that they truly took part in the Battle of Britain and you can take your hat off to them.

There was still a good deal of activity; German

bombers were still coming over and Kent was more or less right in their path. It was very exciting to be one of the team, either on the set or the plotting table, working at considerable speed and feeling that you had a real part to play.

It was exhausting work and the watch system took some getting used to. When we were not short-handed we worked a four-watch system, which was fairly easy: 1-6pm; 8am-1pm; 11pm-8am; 6-11pm, then off duty till 1pm two days later. But if you had to go on a 3-watch system, it was really gruelling; the watches had to be worked by only three groups of people and you only got 24 hours off to recover in. A 3-watch system was dreaded by everyone and I was lucky not to be on one very often. By the time I joined they'd trained almost enough operators to man all the different radar chains. I think it's a lot easier to work either continuous night shifts or continuous day shifts; on a watch system like ours your own system never had time to get adjusted to being up all night.

And it wasn't as if you could sleep like a top when you finally did get your head down. The barrack huts were far too large to allow you to sleep with just your own watch; so you can imagine what happened.

Having been up all night, you'd retire to bed after breakfast, then at noon the 1 o'clock watch would come crashing into the hut to get their "irons" (elegant Government-issue knife, fork, spoon and mug) ready for first-shift lunch. No sooner had you dropped off again after that outburst than the 8-1 watch would come off duty and burst in for *their* irons. Sleep was far from peaceful, and to add to our troubles, very few radar stations had a sitting-room of any sort or description for the ranks. So we were always either on watch or in the Naafi, or in the cookhouse, or in our barrack huts and it was not unusual to have half a dozen girls sitting on their beds or round the stove, chatting away whilst you and the rest of your watch were trying to sleep.

This is one of the things I look back on with amazement now - how little they did to try to make our off-duty life comfortable. I think it was at that time that I developed a lifetime's habit of needing to put my feet up in order to feel that I'm relaxing. Since you spent so much time sitting on your bed, you obviously lay on it instead - biscuits and all - and to this day, as soon as I sit down, I want to put my feet up!

I believe that on big bomber and fighter stations there were more creature comforts and they were better equipped in every way. The radar stations were the cinderellas of the service and ENSA concerts hardly ever came our way. If one did it was usually a third or fourth-rate affair - I never heard of Vera Lynn visiting a radar station!

Although radar had been around for quite a long time, the people who lived near the stations never entirely got used to those tall aerials and were highly suspicious of them. We used to go into Canterbury or Faversham by bus, and the people around us would be warning each other not to go too close to "those big masts" as they'd stop your watch if you did. All sorts of other ways of doing you a mischief were hinted at too ("It's the rays they give out, you know".) In fact we heard rumours that young lovers, before an evening out with their girls, used to go as close as they could to the aerials and deliberately expose themselves to a quick burst in the hopes of making themselves sterile for the evening!

I acquired a boy friend at Dunkirk - one Johnny Johnson. Of course I had one or two other boy friends - nobody stuck to one fellow for very long in those days. But this was my first regular fellow I'd met on a station, and he was the best dancer I ever danced with before or since.

Those were the days of the big bands and swing, and we both adored dancing and used to put records on in the Naafi during off-duty hours and dance to them endlessly. Alternatively, someone would play on the saloon-bar type piano. It was a curious fact that although the stations were very small, with never more than about 150 people on them, there was nearly always some genius who could play really good jazz or boogie on the piano and make the place hum a bit. Often there were one or two other instrumentalists, and they would work up a very satisfactory jam session to cheer our hours off duty.

Anyway, Johnny and I struck up a friendship which - although it never led to anything serious - lasted nevertheless all through the war (though we were only on the same station for a few months) and for many years afterwards, with Christmas cards, photographs of spouses, children etc. I only lost touch with him when he emigrated to New Zealand and sent me a sad little picture postcard from the ship saying "Goodbye now Annie" which quite choked me up. I suppose he thought that Christmas cards from the other side of the world would ruin him in postage!

At the same time as all this was going on, I had another boy friend whom I used to meet from time to time in London when our leaves or passes coincided.

I expect today's young people would be quite shocked

at the total lack of fidelity we showed towards our young men (and they to us!). But it simply was not done in those days to stick like a leech to one fellow, unless and until you became engaged to him. In fact, to try to do anything of the sort was a cast-iron, guaranteed way of frightening him off in double-quick time!

A man was very happy to take you out and about, but he was even happier if he could see that you went out and about sometimes with other men too, otherwise he'd begin to feel trapped, and if there was one thing young men of my day hated, it was to feel trapped! Once he asked you to marry him, of course, it was different. If you agreed, then he submitted happily to the idea of being trapped. But if he *didn't* mention marriage to you, woe betide you if you gave him any impression that he was your property, or that you expected him to give up dating other girls. That was the kiss of death!

And so - although I can refer to Johnny as a "boy friend" (because we did not have a brother-sister type relationship) yet he used to take other girls out and dance with them, and I was perfectly free to go up to London periodically and meet this other chap Gerald.

Gerald was the only rich man I ever went out with. Every girl should have at least one really rich man in her life, to take her out and about and make her feel expensive!

This one was a member of one of the big drink firm families, and he was in a crack cavalry regiment. My father used to mock him, because he'd never been on the back of a horse in his life! He rode a tank instead. He was stationed near enough to London to reach it in about an hour in his flashy Frazer-Nash sports car (any girl's dream) and in summer we'd sometimes go for a picnic in the country, or spend a day on the river and finish up at the Compleat Angler at Marlow, or at one of the many popular roadhouses there were in those days quite close to London, where you could dine and dance, and sometimes even swim.

We would either go alone, or get up a party with two or three other couples. On such occasions, all the men in the party would dance with all the girls; you might certainly have more dances with your own particular fellow, and always the last dance, but it would have been considered the height of bad manners for the others not to dance with you at all. Our social life, in fact, snowballed this way; it was not uncommon to meet a new young man on such an outing, then get a phone call from him a few days later asking you out himself. Just because you'd been at the previous occasion with somebody else, it didn't mean that you were his private property - not by a long chalk!

If Gerald and I were going out for the evening in London, the programme would usually go something like this.

I would check into a hotel (not easy to find a room, but one usually managed) and then hot-foot it along to Elizabeth Arden's place in Bond Street. This dear lady had resolved to make a contribution to the war effort by offering a complete facial and make-up to any girl in uniform for a very low price indeed (I think it was one guinea.) Lots of people made these marvellous gestures during the war (like Lord Nuffield and the sanitary towels!) But Lizzie Arden was even more popular with her offer of a chance to look your very best for an evening out at a price you could actually afford.

So there I'd be, lying back like a duchess in one of

her cubicles, while my face was massaged with all sorts of beautiful creams, and my nails were manicured by somebody else, and finally an expert makeup was applied, and I'd emerge from the shop feeling a new woman.

A long soak in a luxurious hot bath would follow, the silk stocking was removed and the hair allowed to descend to the shoulders, and, in full evening dress, I'd emerge looking unrecognisable as One-oh-eight Miller!

We nearly always started the evening at the Savoy, where the incomparable Caroll Gibbons was at work on that piano, and here we would eat an amazingly good meal. The size of the menu would make the diner-out of today laugh, but quantity is not always quality, and the food was marvellous. There was nothing the matter with the Savoy's wine cellar during the war either, and my young man being in the drink business knew just what to order.

In between courses we danced of course, and then eventually tore ourselves away and "went on" as it was called, to a night club, perhaps the Coconut Grove or the Four Hundred or the Suivi.

I found these places terribly exciting. First you had to be a member (or become one). Then you nearly always descended stairs to reach the club and you could hear the gorgeous music coming up at you, which put you instantly in the right mood. A table would be found, with difficulty as it was always very dark, but eventually you'd settle down and the waiter would bring a bottle with Gerald's name on it (kept from his last visit).

The next hour or so would be spent holding hands, kissing surreptitiously, and dancing on the very small dance floor which required a special technique known as nightclub dancing: you didn't make much progress but your feet kept time to the music and your bodies kept tightly glued together.

Around midnight or so there'd be a cabaret which was usually wonderful. Somebody like "Hutch" would sing "When they begin the beguine" perhaps. (You can still buy a record of him doing it and it still sounds pretty good!)

Later on we'd get hungry and order bacon and eggs and coffee to round the night off – delicious! At last, tired out, we'd call it a night and wend our way back up the stairs and out into the deserted streets, to find dawn breaking over London and a nasty hangover breaking inside your head.

Sometimes I'd get a bit of sleep but often there was only time to get back to the hotel and change into uniform again, get the hair off the collar again, and rush for a train back to camp. Arriving there would be the most awful anti-climax imaginable: after all that glamorous life, to be confronted by a noisy barrack hut full of girls collecting their irons and heading for the cookhouse! *Awful!*

London was a truly wonderful place during the war. It's funny nowadays to hear people grumbling on about "all the foreigners" because during the war it was precisely "all the foreigners" who made it such an exciting, magical place. You'd see from their shoulder flashes where they were from: Poland perhaps, or Free France, or Canada, or Australia, or New Zealand, or of course the good old U.S.of A. They were all so friendly, too. The British people had defrosted almost overnight when war broke out and there was an amazing atmosphere of cameraderie which warmed the cockles of your heart. I loved every moment of it.

So it was a very nasty shock when, after only about six months at Dunkirk, I suddenly got my marching orders and was told to proceed forthwith to a place called Barkway, near Royston in Hertfordshire. And the rumours were rife that this was to be a new kind of radar altogether.

5. "GEE"

Barkway is a very small village near Royston, and the RAF had taken over a big house there belonging to Sir Humphrey de Trafford. There were huts for the "erks" (other ranks) and also for the radar operations, but the morning after I arrived there, I was summoned with the other new arrivals to the big house, where we were interviewed in what had been the drawing-room by a chap with more scrambled eggs on his hat than I'd ever seen before. (Scrambled eggs is service jargon for a lot of gold decoration, signifying senior rank.)

He gave us all a pep talk, explaining that Britain was no longer thinking in terms of "taking it on the chin" but more in terms of "dishing it out". He told us that we were to learn how to operate a different kind of radar, strictly navigational, and that from now on we would be working for Bomber Command, not Fighter Command.

He then did something which I found rather touching. He explained that bombers being in the business of killing people, we might possibly have some kind of conscientious objection to being directly involved in this, and that if any of us had strong feelings about it, we could be excused at this stage and would be returned to the place from whence we came. And no hard feelings.

There was a total hush in the room. Nobody moved and nobody spoke.

Within an hour we were in the classroom learning all about it.

"Gee" was what they called it. Very clever stuff. It had been started in March of 1942 and it worked a bit like lighthouses. Transmitters some distance apart on the ground sent out signals which were picked up by a receiver in the bomber. The set inside the bomber could take a fix from the transmitters, and because it "knew" where they were and knew the time it took for radio waves to travel, it could pinpoint its position on a grid up to a distance of 250 miles. Very simple, really.

In fact, from our point of view it was a lot too simple. It was deadly dull. Our job was to keep watch on the signal and keep it in the correct position. There was a Master station and two or three slave stations connected by intercom to a Monitor. The Monitor's job was to keep watch on the slaves and tell them if the pulse was wandering. A very small wander could cause a very big misconception on the part of the navigator in the bomber.

Oh yes, it was extremely vital work, there's no doubt about that. But after a while we decided that any average monkey could be trained to do it in a day.

There were endless hours of boredom, when absolutely nothing happened and we stared at the cathode ray tube in the darkened ops room with its weird green luminous screen with a big green luminous loop on it. You'd fall into a sort of stupor, then suddenly all hell would break loose when the transmitter "tripped" (went off the air.) It took only a matter of seconds for the spare transmitter to take over but the pulse would be in entirely the wrong place on the screen. So you would suddenly have to galvanise yourself into action, wind all the knobs like mad, and get the thing back in the right place again. Speed was of the essence then, because if a navigator happened to take a fix at that moment, he'd be totally confused as to where he was. So with all the adrenalin going flat out, you'd perform this very simple operation at lightning speed, and then sink back into your previous dreary stupor.

Just about the only job interest which came our way was to glance at the blackboard when you came on watch and note which were the targets. To counteract your boredom you could sit there and picture the bombers approaching Berlin or Frankfurt, the crews relying totally on you for their navigation. This was rewarding, but the work on Gee required nothing like the skill or excitement of CH radar and I missed this a lot.

The only other method of relieving the boredom was chatting up the person on the other end of your intercom. Apart from routine commands passed from one to the other to "come two ohs positive" or negative as the case might be, there was nothing to do but chat and try to keep each other awake during the long night hours. Serious flirtations used to start up this way; but every now and again the two people concerned would arrange to meet each other on a day off and a lot of beautiful illusions would be shattered.

It was essential to keep alert on the set, and because of this and also concern for our eyes, we were allowed on for only an hour at a time. (I often wonder these days about VDU operators who sometimes work on them for hours at a time. The RAF took great care of our eyes.) So the watches were in effect doubled up, and your hour off was spent making endless cups of coffee, knitting, reading, writing letters, or simply chatting, and (in the case of one girl I remember) *tatting!*

On the night watch we'd make ourselves supper, usually eggs and bacon, and we made decent tea and coffee, unlike the notorious Naafi coffee we drank so much of and which tasted of something so unspeakable I'd rather not speak of it. Usually two people were in charge of the "tea swindle" as we called it (probably because we had to swindle it out of the cooks!).

I remember one day, when I was in the wilds of Scotland later on, I got a bit bored with bacon and eggs and scrounged some cheese from the cookhouse to make us a Welsh Rarebit for a change. It turned out disastrously – one of those cheeses which oozes into a gooey toffee when you cook it, and nothing you can do will save it. Everybody made a valiant effort to eat it and pretend they were enjoying it except the mechanics, who rang down from the transmitter block and said thanks very much for the cement we'd sent them, but finding it impossible to eat, they'd stuck it on the transmitter tower! Together with the ubiquitous Mr Chad of course, saying "WOT NO EGGS".

Mr Chad, incidentally, was entirely a radio character. Who invented him I do not know, but he consists of nothing but radio symbols: sine waves, positive and negative signs etc. And the question mark must never be put after the question, but always on top of his head. He was for ever apearing in the most unlikely places on radar stations, asking some extremely funny questions and quite often, rather rude ones!

Since I've touched on the subject of food, I must say that we certainly didn't starve in the forces. We were given the best of whatever was available, always, and I remember hearing once that RAF stations did even better because air crew were entitled to better rations in the nature of their job, and all RAF stations were supplied with air crew rations because it was simpler that way.

So I was lucky and had far more to eat than civilians did. It was probably not a diet to be recommended – lots of stodgy puddings in winter, too much pastry and bread etc. But it was civilians who suffered most through wartime rationing. It's much more difficult to be clever with a weekly quarter pound of marge and two thin rashers of bacon than it is when you're catering for several hundred and get your supplies in bulk. I often used to feel ashamed when I went home on leave and watched my mother trying to cope with the little she had, and I always tried to take chocolate and whatever I could as we had so much more of everything than they did.

But in all respects other than food, home was paradise! The incredible feel of carpets under your feet, of soft chairs to sit on, of your own lovely bed with its mattress all in one piece!

You'd feel completely disoriented at first when you got home: the contrast between the spartan life in camp and the luxury of even the most ordinary of homes was almost too much. Of course you got used to it after a few days, and then it was awful having to go back to camp and get used to all the discomforts again. We may have got the best of the food, but we got the best of very little else!

I've wandered away a bit from my training time at Barkway. But apart from learning a very simple job indeed, there was nothing very memorable about that period, and within quite a short time I was loading up my kitbag once again and setting off on another of those nightmare train journeys – this time to Yorkshire.

6. DANBY BEACON

High up on the Yorkshire moors about equidistant from Middlesbrough and Whitby, there lies a small village with a mostly agricultural community (very like the background pictured so well by James Herriot in his books), called Danby. And from the village you can climb (if you want to) a very steep hill indeed which rises 200 feet at an angle of about one in four to the top of the beacon – Danby Beacon. It must of course be one of the chain of English beacons, so it was a very suitable place to put a radar beacon on the Gee chain.

Radar stations were always sited in very high, isolated places, to achieve maximum range, reduce interference, and to keep them away from populated areas. We all knew by now that we were doomed to spend the rest of the war in these lonely, exposed spots. I dare say some people who love the Yorkshire moors might have considered Danby a wonderful posting, but I heard one or two disgusted Londoners describe the surrounding scenery as "miles and miles of bugger-all".

The beacon was so high that it was often shrouded in mist during the winter months, and the track leading up there from Danby was often impassable by transport in winter, so if you wanted to leave the camp, you left on foot. So you thought twice about leaving, because you also had to climb all the way back up on foot!

We were very isolated indeed, and all the city-bred people hated it. Even I, brought up in the country, found it desolate, cold and bleak; and it was a good job I didn't know then that Danby would merely serve me as a training ground for the next station I would be posted to!

To cheer ourselves up we put on a show. There was a one-act play in the first half and variety in the second. "Hullo Danby, here we come!" we sang to the tune of San Francisco here I come, to start the show off with a burst of enthusiasm. I had a lovely gloomy role in the play, which was all about a family squabbling over a will with the "corpse" upstairs who of course turned out to be alive after all, and who made a dramatic entrance at the end, telling his nearest and dearest exactly what he thought of them. *The Dear Departed* I think it was called.

Our liberty runs consisted of loading up a couple of lorries with two or three dozen people who were not on duty, and driving them over the moors to Whitby or Middlesbrough for an evening on the thrash.

We could go to cinemas or pubs, but there was little else doing in wartime, and soon you were bored even with liberty runs. I used to enjoy the singsong in the back of the lorry on the way home: everybody joined in at the tops of their voices, which made you feel you'd had a good evening, even if you hadn't. All the usual favourites came out for an airing: Nellie Dean, Lily Marlene and her sister Lily of Laguna, Roll out the Barrel, The Quartermaster's Stores. And I must say that most of the men were a gentlemanly lot and restricted themselves to the cleaned-up versions when there were Waafs present.

Very nice of them, I think, and it wasn't until after the war was over that I learned a few of the words they'd probably have preferred to sing and there was even a very rude and funny one describing various anatomical details of Messrs Hitler, Himmler and Goebbels which I eventually learned from my own children about twenty years after the war was over!

I won't pretend that being in the women's forces was particularly good for your vocabulary. We might not have sung terribly rude songs, but we did pick up some pretty basic Anglo-Saxon language from living and working with men all the time, and many must have found it hard to break themselves of what became a habit which would not have been so acceptable in "civvy street". I think I must have shocked my mother many times, and to this day I reckon I could tell you within a few minutes whether a woman of my age had ever served in the ranks. There is something earthy and forthright about her, and she usually smokes. At least if she was on radar, she does. All those hours we had to kill when not on the set encouraged nearly everyone to smoke; there wasn't much else to do, and nobody had told us then that it was dangerous. It was considered a nice sociable custom, and they were so cheap you always handed them round and it was a rare bird indeed who didn't take one. I smoked Players in those days and they were only 1/6d for 20 (7½p)!

Another thing we all did in those days which would be considered dangerous and silly today was to hitchhike all over the country.

I've already explained about train journeys and how time-consuming they could be, and on radar you used to get 36-hour passes which simply couldn't be wasted sitting in stationary trains. While I was at Danby, for instance, my sister and her family were living at Whitley Bay near the submarine base at Blyth, Northumberland. It was no distance at all for me to go and visit her on a 36-hour pass, and I used to hitch quite easily all the way, whereas it would have taken me heaven knows how long by rail.

Service people could travel in service vehicles as well as civilian ones, so as long as you were in uniform you had about ten times as much chance of getting a lift, because there must have been at least ten times more service vehicles on the roads than civilian.

As a matter of fact, we had a lot of fun hitchhiking. You met all sorts of people and they were always garrulous, so you learned all about their life histories in quite a short journey. Lorry drivers are bored and lonely people and delighted to get some company in the cab. I do remember one, however, who wasn't so delighted, when he gave a lift to three of us girls, one of whom weighed about 12 stone.

He was driving a civilian lorry with a large notice in the cab reminding him that giving lifts was forbidden. He stopped nevertheless, and the outsize Waaf seated herself on the engine casing in the cab beside the driver, which presently gave way to her weight with an awful loud denting noise. The driver slammed his brakes on and an emergency baling-out operation ensued; he just couldn't get rid of us fast enough! I wonder what on earth he said when he got back to his depot; apart from a large human body there was very little else which could have explained that dent!

Most people went out of their way to help a girl in uniform, and sometimes a long way out of their way. Only lack of petrol would prevent the average civilian from literally turning round and going in the opposite direction if they could help you to get home on leave a little more quickly. Nothing, but nothing was too much trouble if it could help us on our way. And I never once heard of any girl being attacked or bothered by anybody when hitchhiking, even alone.

While I was at Danby I had my twenty-first birthday. My father organised the whole thing. He'd been commanding an anti-aircraft training regiment, at Blandford in Dorset, but by that time his regiment at Blandford had been disbanded (much to his grief), supposedly because by then they'd trained enough anti-aircraft gunners.

He'd been posted to the Gunner Depot at Woolwich, which, being rather a dangerous place to live, had meant moving my mother to a house in Sevenoaks.

So he laid on a private dinner in the mess for me, with my two parents, my sister and her husband, and the aforementioned boyfriend Johnny Johnson. There was by chance a huge garrison dance on that night and it had been one of my father's pleasanter duties at the Depot to form a dance band. He'd managed to get together about twenty first-class professional dance band musicians and had them posted to Woolwich and he was extremely proud of them.

So we sat down to a remarkably good dinner, at which I was embarrassed to be waited on by ATS girls of the same rank as myself, but since we were in evening dress, I hoped they didn't realise it. Afterwards we all went on to the dance, and of course the band played Happy Birthday to me and Twenty-One Today, and I was allowed to ask them to play any tune I wanted for the whole evening. It was wonderful, especially as I had Johnny to dance with.

A strange incident occurred at the end of that evening – so strange I think it worth telling here. On the way back to Sevenoaks in the train, my sister suddenly noticed that I'd lost an earring. I was sad, as they were pretty and quite valuable antique ones. My father, when he heard about it, had notices stuck up all over the place, and notified the taxi driver, but alas, to no effect.

One year later that taxi driver was clearing out his garage (obviously not a regular performance). Sweeping out all the debris of a year, in amongst the dust and the dead autumn leaves, he spotted my earring, completely undamaged. As if that wasn't enough, he remembered my father's name and promptly phoned him at the Depot, and that pair of earrings is still at this moment lying safely in my drawer! Happy ending!

Not long after this I was posted yet again. This time it was Scotland I was to head for.

It was one of the more difficult aspects of service life that you never seemed to be given long enough on each station; no sooner had you settled in and made some friends than they posted you away, and quite soon you'd almost forgotten all their names.

7. WINDYHEAD HILL

High up above the North Sea on the coast of Aberdeenshire, there is a peak clearly marked on the ordinance survey maps "Windyhead Hill". If you've ever heard a Scotsman understating the subject of the weather, you will realise that this must have been a very windy hill indeed for them to have given it such a name. It meant that to a Sassenach it was exposed to all the elements and unfit for human habitation.

I'd thought that Danby was pretty desolate, but believe me I had experienced nothing there, except possibly a useful sort of run-up to Windyhead Hill. The nearest village was New Aberdour and the nearest railway station was Strichen – a very apt name for it.

I suppose in summer it was rather beautiful up there on that headland; in fact I have in recent years paid it a sort of respectful, nostalgic visit, and found to my surprise that it was.

Why is it then, I wonder, that I remember so little of the summer up there, but that every detail of the winter months is etched into my mind for ever more?

When they constructed that camp, they hadn't thought things out very carefully. There was the usual steep uphill climb from the living site to the radar site, which was at least a mile away in case the radar was attacked from the air.

But at Windy there was also a quite unnecessary walk from the sleeping huts to the "ablutions". So if you were on the bath rota one wild and stormy night in mid-January, you had to put on your oilskins, sou'wester and gumboots over your pyjamas, just in order to fight your way back through the blizzard to your bed. And the same sort of thing applied if you had to get up in the night to spend a penny. I expect the men just did it out of the window, but that, for a woman, would have resulted in unthinkable injury!

The very fact that we were issued, on arrival, with thick black oilskins, sou'westers and wellingtons was enough to rouse suspicion instantly. Clearly, if the RAF thought we were going to need them, we were going to need them!

In fact there were times in winter when no form of transport could have taken us up that hill to go on watch, and so, some nights, a Waaf dressed up to kill in her oilskins, weighed down with the tea swindle, knitting, etc, could not get herself up that hill either! On such occasions, the boys of the RAF Regiment (whose proper function was to guard us) used to be detailed, two to a Waaf, to push and pull us up the hill until we were safely inside the Ops block! In a full gale, your oilskin, which was very stiff (ask any lifeboatman) acted as a sort of sail, and you could easily have taken off and sailed off over the edge of the cliff if you hadn't had those chaps to hold you down.

The conditions were often really appalling, and there were times when we found ourselves sobbing with sheer exhaustion trying to fight the elements.

We did, however, have one or two compensations at Windy. We were lucky to have a really good Commanding Officer, who obviously realised how difficult life was for the girls under his care, and who leaned over backwards to try to make it more endurable for us.

I myself decided after a while that God helps those who help themselves, and made up my mind to get up a camp concert party. I advertised on the notice board for talent – any sort of talent, and after a slow start, people began to come forward offering their little party pieces, and in no time at all we had rehearsals under way.

I'd always nursed a sneaking ambition to be a great stage producer, so here was my chance. Imagine my consternation when one day, at rehearsal, I was approached by a sergeant in the RAF Regiment – very good-looking fellow – who diffidently offered to do a couple of Dickens sketches for us. It turned out he was a professional actor in peacetime and I promptly felt all the Cecil B. de Mille in me evaporating fast.

I offered to hand the whole thing over to him, but he'd have none of it, saying that it was my show and I must get on with it. He just joined the rest of the cast, and did a most marvellous Uriah Heep monologue for us which was so good that there was a real danger of him showing up the complete amateurishness of the rest of us. He made himself up beautifully, and the rather handsome young man would vanish utterly and in his place would appear this wizened, crafty-looking old man, rubbing his mittened hands together and croaking about being "a very 'umble man, used to eating 'umble pie".

For the next few weeks we divided our time between staring into our cathode ray tubes while the huge bomber raids escalated over Germany, and rehearsing our little show like mad, which wasn't too easy with the cast all working different hours.

Here the C.O. helped, allowing us to get watches changed so that as many of us as possible could be off duty at the same time. An example of how helpful he always was; in fact he was so keen on the show he even took part in it himself, giving a very spirited rendering of "Caviare Comes from the Virgin Sturgeon" which brought the house down. Then we had an appealing Scottish lass who sang "Cuddle up a little closer" in a very fetching way. There was a small band; the usual talented jazz pianist; one or two topical and parochial sketches we'd written ourselves; a short but heart-rending drama; a serious violinist – in fact a bit of everything.

At last we put the show on – three or four performances so that all watches could see it. They seemed to enjoy it enormously, but I doubt if they enjoyed it half as much as we enjoyed rehearsing and performing it.

Next thing we knew, our fame had spread abroad somehow or other (I always suspected the C.O.) because we were invited to put the whole show on at Dyce, a nearby bomber station.

I was absolutely terrified. Here we would have a very different setup: about 2,000 personnel on the station (instead of about 150) and we'd have to perform in one of the huge hangars, and there'd be catcalls and probably boos. It was one thing getting up a little show like that for ones own friends in a nice cosy atmosphere where everybody wanted it to be good; but in front of a thousand strangers it was an entirely different matter. This was the kind of station where they *did* get Vera Lynn, and their standards would be a whole lot higher!

There was no getting out of it, though, and the day finally dawned. Before we piled into the lorries, some of us had a cup of coffee in the Naafi to steady our nerves. When we climbed aboard, with the band instruments taking up a lot of room, especially the drum which somebody kept thumping, I began to feel rather ill. I realised what a terrible mistake I'd made – Naafi coffee always had a ghastly effect on my digestive tract, and my nerves were piling on the agony.

The C.O. noticed I was in a state and decided the only cure for it was gin. Neat gin. He passed me a flask and I swallowed some. It actually made me feel far worse, but I kept on having a swig because he was so utterly confident that it'd do the trick.

The indigestion got worse but the gin did have the effect of deadening my stage fright, and I remember very little about the performance that night. I can recall the huge hangar, with a thick pall of smoke swirling in the footlights and a sea of grinning faces beyond, but after a time we realised they were actually grinning with pleasure, not mocking us, and everybody seemed to be thoroughly enjoying themselves. We received huge applause plus catcalls (but not derisory ones – approving ones) and we rounded off a successful evening with a really stirring sing-song.

Huge sing-songs like that during the war were wonderful. Wars always seem to inspire these grand songs to sing, and everybody loves to belt them out. There were the defiant ones about Hanging out the washing on the Siegfried Line; the songs of yearning for Bluebirds over the White Cliffs of Dover; romantic songs about Nightingales singing in Berkeley Square; Vera Lynn's We'll Meet Again; and the straight belt-'em-out songs like Roll out the Barrel. Devotees of Dad's Army heard some of them; they used to weave nostalgically in and out of the programme and jog your memory back over the years. Everyone loved them and loved periodically to open up their lungs and really raise the roof.

You never hear people sing like that in civilian life and probably not in peacetime at all; it takes a war to fill the hearts with that sort of special fervour. We didn't sound like King's College choir, but I'll bet we could have brought a lump to your throat just the same.

And that's how that "request performance" came to an end, and at last, flushed with our own success and in my case with gin as well, we piled back into our transports and that was the last of my little concert party.

There were other, more routine, amusements of course, such as the camp dance which took place periodically in the Naafi. Our own little band would play, and beer could be bought, and there was even a peculiar thing called a "dhu strath" which was a huge, heather-filled hollow on the edge of camp, where young men and maidens used to disappear on summer evenings during dances. We even had our own version of a popular song which went "Roll me over in the dhu-strath" which was rather silly really, since it didn't rhyme like clover does.

Our C.O. had worked out a strange little ploy on dance nights which became rather a pleasant tradition. Knowing full well how much his Waafs missed their home comforts and how much genuine hardship we endured up there in winter, he used to choose two or three girls on dance nights and invite them into the Officer's Mess at the end of the evening for a drink. It was considered an honour to be asked, and he used to share the honours out equally among us.

There were only about four or five officers on a radar camp, and I dare say the C.O. got a bit sick of their faces and welcomed a few new ones about the place for a change.

It was inevitable that when it finally got round to my turn to be invited, it all ended in tears; and this is the little story I promised you earlier to illustrate why Waaf Admin. Officers were not always terribly popular.

I believe there was very little love lost between the C.O. and that particular Waaf officer, and I think she must have been stewing up her dislike of him and planning ways and means of making trouble. The fact remained, though, that she had sat by and watched these regular invasions of the mess for a good long time and done nothing about them whatever. It was undeniable that we were off limits when we were in the mess; no Other Ranks were allowed in unless they were cleaning or serving food. Everyone knew the rule and everyone appreciated the C.O's ignoring of it on these rare occasions.

You can picture our horror, therefore, when on the morning after my visit there, I and the other girls were all told that we were to be put on a charge for being out of bounds the night before!

Of all the crazy things to do! The whole camp was thunderstruck. We were told to parade in front of the lady herself at noon (caps orf, 'ef, roi, 'ef, roi) and when we got in there, we found that she had produced a witness in order to back up her case (of all the daft things, when she herself had seen us there and talked to us and accepted a cup of coffee from my own hands!)

By the time my turn came, I was so fed up I decided to try a touch of the barrack-room lawyer stuff, and said I wanted to call a witness myself - the C.O.

"Ma'am" went scarlet in the face and told us that

there would be a recess and we were to go. Next thing we knew, we were all called back after lunch and the C.O. was sitting there himself, and he proceeded to make a very humble and contrite apology to us, to "Ma'am", and to the world in general, declaring that he had been entirely in the wrong to invite us there, and that it would not happen again in the future.

And it never did. The charge was dropped and our little bit of innocent pleasure on dance nights was at an end from that day on.

Just about our only other diversion at Windy was to walk down the road a mile or so to the village pub at New Aberdour. It was a very humble, almost a spit-and-sawdust pub, and apart from having a drink, there were only two amusements: playing darts and shocking the natives.

In the early 1940s, it was still almost unheard of for women to be seen in pubs in Scotland. This may be hard to believe now, but it was a fact; even in Aberdeen, I've been among a party entering a bar and been asked to leave (the women, that is.) We would comply with these requests, because it was the custom of the country and we had very little choice, but we were always indignant. Pubs didn't open on a Sunday at all.

But down in our local village I'm afraid we adopted a fairly tough attitude; there was so little for us to do in our time off that we simply decided to ignore all this nonsense and "press on regardless". The locals used to sit huddled in a corner, mostly old men, showing their disapproval very plainly; but we just paid no attention, and even (horror of horrors!) quite often went in unaccompanied by a male!

I mentioned that I've since paid a return visit to Windy, and I located the pub in question and we went in there for a drink. Of course it's quite unrecognisable now, pleasantly modernised and with even a well-patronised dining-room! I told the landlord about those old days, and some of the men present were listening, and they all laughed when I told them what it had been like, and how we Waafs had been the pioneers who had braved the disgust of the local men of those villages. I doubt if some of them believed a word I was saying!

I was also fascinated to find, on my return visit, that there were still aerials on top of that windswept hill, and on knocking rather nervously at the door of the building beside the masts, I found a coastguard there. We had a long chat, and he admitted that he wouldn't like at all to have to live up there as well as work; of course he went happily off to his nice warm, comfortable home at the end of his spell of duty. He also told me that I was by no means the first woman who'd called there on such a pilgrimage; there had been one or two before me, ex-Waafs, who'd also dragged their husbands all the way there and regaled them with hair-raising and scarcely-to-be-believed 'line-shoots' about what life had been like for them there during the war. There'd even been one who'd come all the way from Canada!

I said to him, "Well, isn't it true, the way we describe it?" and he admitted that it's quite unspeakable up there in winter time.

We used to have liberty runs to Fraserburgh and watch the fishing boats coming in with their catches, which was nice, and we occasionally got as far as Aberdeen.

What I remember best about Aberdeen, though, was arriving there after the ghastly all-night journey from London after being on leave, and crossing the road to a wonderful place right opposite the station where you could get a really princely Scottish-style breakfast, even in those wartime days. Oatcakes, drop scones, baps, porridge, bacon and eggs, decent coffee – it was marvellous, and how they did it all through the war, I can't imagine. It was tremendously popular with all of us in uniform, especially after those awful night journeys.

Mind you, we didn't fare too badly at Windyhead; I came upon our menu for Christmas 1943 and reproduce it here:

R.A.F. WINDYHEAD HILL
XMAS, 1943

Cream of Tomato Soup.

Fried Fillets of Sole.
Lemon Sauce.

Roast Turkey (Stuffed),
Braised sausages,
Cranberry sauce.

Roast Loin of Pork.
Apple sauce.

Parsnips, Brussels Sprouts,
Creamed potatoes,
Baked Potatoes.

Plum Pudding. Rum sauce.

Biscuits and cheese.

Coffee.
Fruit.
Cigarettes.

BEER
MINERALS

and the signatures from the back of it:

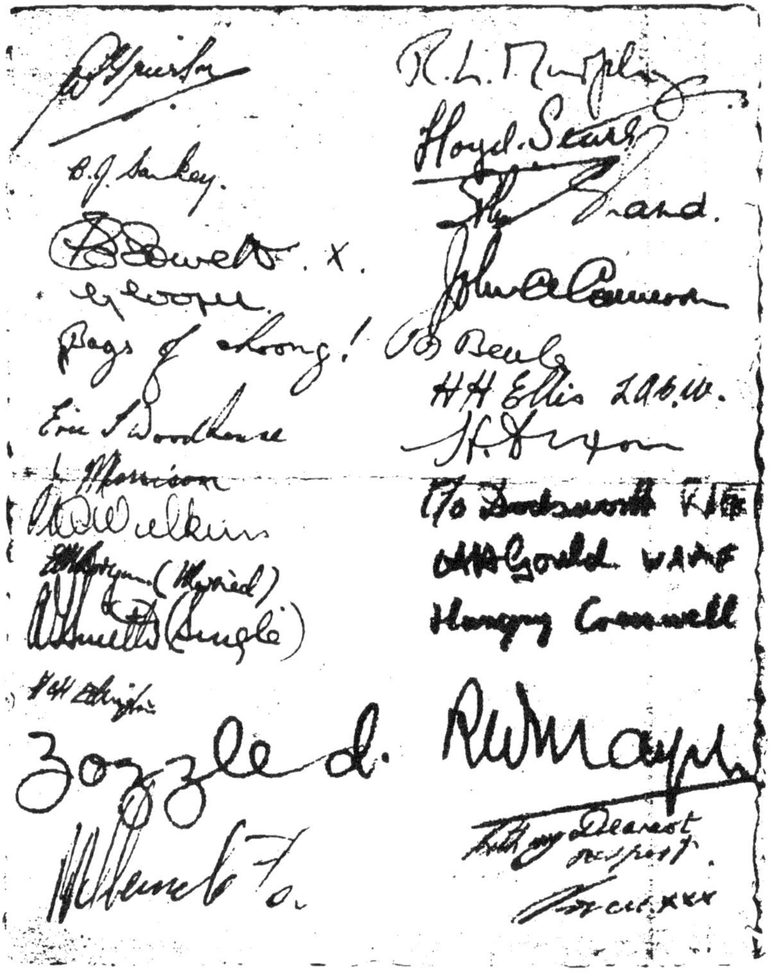

We always did ourselves proud on Burns Night, too. The C.O., though English, believed that when in Rome you do as the Romans do, and he saw to it that the whole station joined in the big occasion, with proper haggises and a proper piper to pipe them in, and proper Scotsmen to recite the regulation yards and yards of proper Burns poetry in a properly incomprehensible accent! Followed, of course, by the regulation toast to The Immortal Memory.

On the whole, I think that although Windy was far and away the toughest place I was ever stationed on, and the life we led was almost unbelievably hard at times, it was nevertheless the happiest station I was on and the one I remember most clearly after all these years.

And I think we had the C.O. to thank for that; a happy ship is always thanks to its captain. He was a marvellous character, and strangely enough I was destined to meet him again, about twenty years later.

I was shopping in my home town Saturday market, when I spotted his familiar face – not much changed. He was a big, good-looking chap even then, and he stood there with an enormous cauliflower under his arm, staring at me as I stared at him.

"I KNOW YOU!", he said. And I said, "Yes, I was one of your Waafs at Windy" (I nearly said Sir.) He said, "My God, yes, I thought you must have been! But there were so many, you must forgive me that I can't put a name to you" (as if he possibly could.)

I told him and then reminded him of the incident of the out-of-bounds charge. He fairly shouted with laughter and said he remembered it all very clearly. We had a long chat, and I asked him what he did now. "I'm headmaster of .... Grammar School", he said, and I thought to myself what a very happy school it must be, if he ran it like he used to run that RAF camp so long ago.

8. "LORAN"

So I was quite sad when I had to leave Windy, but I was not to leave Scotland yet. My next posting was not far away, to Cruden Bay a little further south down the east coast of Aberdeenshire. And when I arrived, I learned that it was "something experimental".

It was, in fact, an American brain-child. The main shortcoming of Gee as a navigational aid over Europe was the fact that by the time the bombers arrived over Germany, the lines of the actual grid by which the navigator took his fix were getting very far apart, and it was difficult for him to pinpoint his position, or that of the target, with very great accuracy. The closer to England he was, the closer the lines of the grid, because that was where the signal emanated from. But if you wanted accurate bombing, you wanted the accuracy over the target, and this problem had been exercising the boffins for quite some time.

There was also the problem of the jamming of Gee, which the Germans were getting too good at.

The Americans had come up with what they hoped was the answer – Loran, which meant Long Range. It was considered to be possible for two important reasons.

One was the fact that from around dusk a thing called the ionosphere condenses around the earth, about 60 miles up, and it is possible to bounce radio waves off this ionosphere and back to earth again some distance away. (You can't send them far by the direct route, because the curvature of the earth gets in the way.)

The other factor which made it feasible was the fact that we had by then got control of North Africa.

The idea was to set up a pair of stations, one in Britain and the other in North Africa (Bizerta in fact), and thus increase the accuracy of the grid over Germany where it was wanted. Our bombers would be able to carry the Gee equipment and Loran as well, and could start out their journey navigating on Gee and then switch to Loran when they got nearer the target area; thus enjoying the maximum accuracy of both grids.

It was a beautiful idea. If only it had worked! Unfortunately, what they hadn't bargained for was the tremendous amount of interference which accompanies the presence of the ionosphere. Everyone knows that when you start twiddling the dial of your radio in the evening, you can pick up so many stations that it's often difficult to settle on the one you really want. Nowadays, of course, equipment has improved and accuracy, even after dusk, is much better. I am told that Loran does work now and survives to this day, probably using satellites instead of the ionosphere.

But in those days, the interference was too much for it, and we spent weeks up there on the cold Scottish east coast, watching a set which presented a picture of something resembling your television set when you switch to a spare channel! Every now and then, almost before you had time to notice it, you could detect in amongst all the mess a fuzzy-looking pulse, but usually it was gone before you had time to recognise it properly, and as for trying to keep it positioned with any accuracy, well it just wasn't on.

It was just my luck to get involved with it! I spent a couple of extremely boring months at Cruden Bay, straining my wretched eyes at this terrible jumble on the screen, often imagining I could see Bizerta when I probably couldn't, and playing Ouija throughout the night with the rest of the watch, who developed a craze for it.

It was all night work, or course; there was no question of picking up Bizerta during the daytime, when the ionosphere is over 90 miles away and gets so thin that most of the radio waves just shoot straight through it.

So we were off all day and on all night, and there were only a very few of us involved in this thing at all. We used to go nearly silly with boredom, and one night somebody turned a tumbler upside down and encircled it with the letters of the alphabet and we started 'getting in touch with the other side'.

Of course, we got terribly bitten with this silly caper. Everyone believed in it implicitly and we made it tell us exactly who was going to get married and who to and when, and how many children they'd have. Every now and again we'd glance at the scribbly mess on the set to make quite sure a miracle hadn't taken place, but it never had, and we could give our full attention to the more important messages which the tumbler was spelling out for us with the help of

"Bridie" who was our usual contact.

I can't remember just how long it took the Powers that Be to decide that Loran wasn't going to work – at least not at that time – but in due course they did so and I was packing up my troubles in my old kitbag once again.

This time I was to head for Dorset, an altogether kinder climate, which by now I felt I richly deserved. Of course it was entirely typical of the war that my parents were no longer living in Dorset. Blandford would have been nice and close to Swanage, where I was now going.

While they'd been there, I used to have some very good times when I went on leave. The dramatic transformation from One-oh-Eight Miller, the lowest form of human life, into the Colonel's daughter was really very funny.

I used to go to the regimental dances quite often; the best of these were always the Sergeant's Mess dances, where they used to treat me rather like a princess, and tell me nice things about my father which were good to hear (whatever their motive), and buy me gins and limes (the popular drink with young people in those days) and generally spoil me rotten.

I think before we wander off to my next station I must digress for a minute and tell you one or two things about my family in general, and my father in particular ...

* * *

My father was an Old Contemptible, having actually sailed to France in March 1914, and been in the retreat from Mons, the battles of Le Cateau, The Marne, First Ypres, Loos, and then Mesopotamia. After the war it was India for a few years and then, before he was forty, he decided to retire and go and hunt in Buckinghamshire. This little idyll didn't last very long, though, because the 1929 crash hit him very hard and he had to sell the house, the hunters and a lot else, and live much more modestly.

But of course he had seen the second war coming, and started pestering the War Office to take him back, which at last they decided to do. He was to report to Blandford on September 3rd 1939 – an appropriate day to don uniform again for the first time after eighteen years!

That day is not one I shall forget. We decided to drive him down to Dorset from Berkhamsted where we lived, and return the same day in the car which we would be needing but he wouldn't.

We called en route at his sister's house at Goring, just in time to hear Neville Chamberlain's solemn broadcast. It was very solemn indeed; so of course my sister and I got the giggles, which we always used to do when we were nervous.

Everybody was horrified – they'd been through a terrible war already and knew that there was nothing funny about it. I'm ashamed to record that we also got the giggles later on when we arrived at the camp in Blandford and were greeted by all the sentries with their monumentally exaggerated salutes – the kind that *tremble*! We had never seen our father in uniform before, or being saluted or anything, and we found it very comical. He got furious and told us to “pull ourselves together and behave”.

We left him there, in that tented camp (which would not be tented for long), and set off on our long drive back to Hertfordshire. It must have been at least 7 0’clock by the time we reached home, and there we found two things waiting for us.

One was a large official notice pinned to the front door warning us that blackouts must be erected at the windows before any lights were switched on.

And the other was the Pepperberg family – mother and two children aged six and four – sitting forlornly on the front doorstep waiting to be let in. Evacuees, from the east end of London! The Billeting Officer had just dumped them there, not even knowing if we’d be coming home to let them in!

We were shattered. Tired and hungry as we were, the blackout business alone would have been bad enough. Nobody’s curtains were light-proof, and something would have to be improvised, and improvised fast. But the Pepperbergs were going to take even more improvising: with beds to make, and a meal to find for them.

We set to work with grim desperation; my mother to cook a meal for twice the number of people she’d bargained for, while my sister and I tried to pin blankets over windows and make up beds. We felt as sorry for the Pepperberg family as we did for ourselves, and my sister, trying to cheer them up, decided to play her record of The Lambeth Walk, hoping it’d make them feel at home! It didn’t of course, and they were pretty miserable.

My mother got on the phone to the billeting officer

next day and explained that we would be packing up and letting our house, probably for the duration of the war, and would like them moved.

"Impossible!" he replied, "your name is down for three evacuees and three evacuees you must have!" (The war provided a perfect breeding-ground for bureaucracy, and local officials like this sprang up like mushrooms overnight, and thoroughly enjoyed chucking their weight about.)

Eventually the Pepperbergs left of their own accord, having decided that the phoney war was here to stay, and back they went to London. I hope they evacuated those children later on, when the war in London wasn't phoney any more.

Quite soon we found a furnished house in Blandford and my father was promoted from second-in-command to Colonel of his regiment.

He loved being back in the Army again. I remember how well he rose to the occasion when a contingent of men evacuated from Dunkirk arrived for a brief rest after their ordeal. My father never left the camp during those days. He turned his own men out of their barrack rooms and made them sleep on the Naafi floor. Their guests were allowed to sleep for 24 hours and were then fed on the best that the cookhouse could provide for them. Nothing was too good for them. Cigarettes were doled out, chocolate, beer – all they could want.

They were finally kitted out and taken by transports to the station where the regimental band played in their honour and a platoon of men from the home camp was lined up to present arms to them as they entrained. My father said afterwards that he'd never seen men in such a terrible state of exhaustion. And he had seen some ...

Another trauma in my father's life at Blandford came when he learned that they were sending him WOMEN!!! The very *idea* of it! His language was unprintable. He came home and swore at my mother and swore at the dog and swore at me and declared that the War Office had gone mad. Whoever heard of women manning ack-ack guns?

The War Office paid no attention and in due course his first batch of ATS arrived. They were not to man the guns, but the predictors, which laid the guns. And to everybody's astonishment, they turned out to be extremely good at it. The men thought the world of them in no time at all, and in the end so did my father! As the weeks passed he began to tell little stories, full of pride, and when the first cadre of girls was trained and ready to leave, and the passing out parade was held, you should have heard my father then!

"My girls were *magnificent*!" he bellowed. "Marched like the Guards! Beat the men into a cocked hat! Never been so proud in me life!"

And he never noticed my mother smiling quietly to herself – far too tactful to remind him of his earlier opinions of girl gunners.

He remained in command of his training regiment until it was disbanded in 1943, and I think it was probably the happiest time of his life. It was also one of the most solvent! For the first time in years he managed to get to grips with his overdraft; he received command pay in addition to his pay as a Lieutenant-Colonel; both his daughters were off his hands, and things were looking unusually rosy.

But not for long of course! The army has an unfortunate little trick of promoting people only to demote them again at the drop of a hat whenever it suits them. They have all sorts of weird terminology to cover this trick: "War Substantive" rank; "Brevet"; or even "Temporary Acting Unpaid".

Amazing! Can you imagine in civilian life somebody being promoted to "Temporary Acting Unpaid Sales Manager" only to be demoted at a moment's notice whenever it suited the company? Ridiculous.. Yes, but they get away with it in the Army.

So what they said in effect, when they wound up his Regiment, was "Thanks very much old boy; you've trained a lot of gunners for us and now we don't need any more, and we don't need any more Lieutenant-Colonels either; so back you go to the Depot and back you go to major!" A bit crushing to the morale this, and devastating to the overdraft; even more so when the Inland Revenue came in on the act. They chose this time to write and inform him that they'd miscalculated his tax throughout the period he'd been at Blandford and he owed them £300!

Of course he didn't take this lying down. The language was positively ear-blistering, and he embarked on a mammoth and protracted private war of his own against His Majesty's Inspector of Taxes. Needless to say he lost. But not without an epic struggle; I believe at one stage he actually took them to court! But all to no avail; he had to start paying back the £300 (a lot of money in those days) when his income had dropped dramatically.

He was always a fighter, my father. He was a typical 'Bateman' colonel type, and on the golf course in peacetime he could be heard three fairways off, yelling at his golf ball, himself, his wife, his daughters and his dog with equal vigour.

They don't seem to breed them quite like that any more.

9. MORE POSTINGS

My next port of call was to a little place called Worth Matravers, near Swanage. I found myself in that area a few months ago, and we visited the little pub in that village which must be one of the most unchanged and least updated pubs in the country. Still quite primitive, but oh how lovely it is, and the landlord there actually managed to dig out an old photograph he had of the radar station as it was when I was there in 1944!

It was not a very eventful posting for me, and I remember less about it than any other station I was on. I couldn't even remember where we lived until my friend the landlord told me we were billeted in a school in Swanage.

I was back on the old Gee again, and I do remember hot summer days on watch when we were actually able to lie in the grass outside the Ops block and sunbathe during our alternate hours off the set.

Of course the beach at Swanage was mined and barricaded so there was little joy in being on the coast; to someone like me who loves the sea so much it was tantalising to see it glittering invitingly in the sun and be unable to answer its invitation. One could walk along the sea front and watch all the shipping out at sea and breathe in the ozone, but it wasn't the same thing at all.

I was there for the time of D-Day, and I can remember all the troop movement that was going on at that time for weeks beforehand, and of course everyone knew invasion was imminent. But that didn't spoil the feeling of profound joy we all felt when our own armies set foot on enemy soil again; or the pride we had in the amazing tactical feats which were accomplished for it, such as the Mulberry Dock, and PLUTO (pipe line under the ocean, to keep the petrol flowing in the most efficient and economical manner.) We who worked on radar had always been proud of British technology, though not actually surprised, for in those days we were used to Britain leading the world.

I was still down there for Christmas and I spent it with the Yanks! I had got acquainted with a G.I. which led to my being invited to their Christmas dinner (imagine being allowed guests!)

It was such an enormous station that they had to do the thing in about four sittings, and it must have been about 5 or 6 o'clock before our turn came round and we'd spent the entire preceeding three or four hours in the bar! Which accounts for the fact that I remember little about it now, except that it was a veritable banquet, and even our excellent Christmas meal the year before at Windyhead was put into the shade. Where the Yanks got all that food from, goodness knows – their magic PX Store I suppose. But remember there was no frozen food in those days.

I'm glad they had a good time that Christmas; for many of them it was their last. They went over to France very soon afterwards, and I heard that a lot of them had been killed, including my pal.

I think they'd probably been training at Weymouth or somewhere for the landings, but I wouldn't have dreamed of asking him, any more than he'd have asked me what went on at my radar site. We were all deeply indoctrinated in the idea that careless talk really did cost lives.

Not long after Christmas I was posted yet again. Pity, because I liked it down at Swanage and it would have been nice to stay somewhere for a little longer.

I often wonder who actually decided all these postings: why one insignificant little Leading Aircraftswoman should be sent to one station, and another to another. Did they do it with a pin, or was there some Deep Inscrutable Plan behind it all?

This time I headed back to Barkway near Royston, where I'd first been trained on Gee.

It was 1945, and this was to be my last posting. And it wasn't a bad one at all because by then my mother had gone to live with her sister at Hoddesden, near Hertford, which was no distance away. This meant that I could actually get home quite often on a 36-hour pass. Royston to Hoddesden, along the Ware road, is a straight run of 25 or so miles, and was a very good example of how useful hitchhiking could be. If I'd tried to get home any other way it would have meant the train to London, endless waiting for a connection, and another train to Hertford. It could have taken half a day or more, easily; whereas by road it was less than an hour.

So a rather amusing situation developed whereby my mother (who didn't like me hitchhiking at all) used actually to walk down to the main road with me and see me off! We would eye the first vehicle which came along and she'd say, "No, not that one, there's only a man on his own in it and I don't like the look of him!" Until a nice respectable-looking family car with a middle-aged couple in it came along and she'd say, "All right, try them!" and if they stopped and picked me up, she'd see me safely into the car and chat the people up a bit: "Now do look after my daughter for me, won't you!"which would make me cringe with embarrassment.

My very dear mother! How she had to adapt in those wartime years! But she adapted very well indeed – probably due to the fact that she and all her generation had already had to learn to adapt only 25 years earlier for another world war.

I was on a Monitor at Barkway, which meant that we were on receiver sets, observing pulses from Master and Slaves. We had no transmitter or signal of our own, merely acting as watchdogs on the other stations. As such, it was even more dreary for us as a job; we didn't even have the occasional excitement of a transmitter trip to cope with. When one of the others had a trip, we would just have to sit there watching for the signal to return to our screen and start moving frantically along to its allotted spot, whereupon we would instruct them to "come two ohs positive" or negative as the case may be. I reckon the P.G.Tips chimps could have picked it up in a day!

Apart from occasional visits to Cambridge, which were marvellous, there wasn't much to do in our spare time. Of course we were not short-handed any more as all the operators they could possibly need had been trained by then, so we were not called upon to go on a 3-watch system or anything terrible like that.

Suddenly it began to dawn on us that the end of the war in Europe might well be in sight. The Allies were racing towards Berlin, and it seemed at long last as if we really were going to win. Not, I should add, that any of us had ever really doubted it for one moment. Even in our very darkest hours it never seriously entered our heads that the Nazis would beat us. Astonishing, really, when you think that they had beaten nearly every other country in Europe!

So about this time, we began discussing (in the rest room during our hours off the set) what we'd do when the war did end, and it was then that I began to learn a few rudimentary political lessons which came as a considerable shock to me.

Very few of us had ever voted in a General Election – the last one had taken place in 1935 and most of us had been too young. I don't think I'd really given politics one moment's serious thought in my life. By upbringing I suppose I was a Tory, but I wasn't consciously anything at all, except a devoted admirer of Winston Churchill, whom I quite reasonably believed had saved our bacon, our honour and our lives.

Imagine my astonishment, therefore, when a lot of my fellow radar operators (especially the men) began talking about the first election we would have after the war was over, and how they were all going to vote Labour.

"Labour!" I said. "But why Labour?"

It seemed they were all thoroughly dissatisfied with the way things had been run before the war, and were determined that we were not going back to that state of affairs after it was over.

"But what about Winston?" I asked. "Are you just going to throw him out after all he's done?"

"Too bad about Winston," they replied, "but he's a Conservative, and we aren't having the Conservatives in power after this lot's over."

I was a bit stunned. But I suppose I'd had what you might call a 'privileged' upbringing and although in many ways I'd received a very good education, yet it hadn't included much in the political field, and I was shamefully ignorant.

When I look back now, I really feel ashamed. I believe that young people today are miles better informed politically and socially, and are also taught to think for themselves about such things much more than we were. If I'd gone to university, it would probably have been different, and I wouldn't have been such an ignoramus.

My degree course in politics took place during the long hours of the night watches in a radar ops room, and it was quite a rude awakening. They all talked of what they considered had been wrong with this country in the thirties, and about what they were going to do to put it right. And they were unanimous in believing that only Labour would be able to do it. So the result of the post-war election came as no surprise to me at all.

Then, on May 8th, I was on the six to midnight watch.

The radio was on in the ops room and suddenly a voice told us to stand by for an important announcement. Everyone came through from the rest room and crowded round the radio, and then we heard those almost incredible words telling us that Germany had laid down her arms in unconditional surrender, and the war in Europe was over.

We were completely stunned, even though we'd been expecting it. Stunned and elated. We came off watch soon after, and as we walked down towards the sleeping camp, it suddenly dawned on us that we were probably the only people who knew!

We stopped in our tracks and the realisation came over us of what a huge secret we carried, and how they were all sleeping innocently in their beds, knowing nothing about it!

I remember very distinctly that it was I who had the bright idea of waking them all up! Everyone looked a bit dubious, and said, "How?"

"By ringing the fire bell!" I cried. "We'll ring it and ring it and ring it and they'll all wake up in a panic and come running out to see what's happening, and we'll tell them we've WON THE WAR!!"

Some of the others thought this was much too daring.

"We'll get into awful trouble," they said. "We're not allowed to touch that fire bell," etc etc, but luckily most of them were not so chicken-hearted and agreed that we couldn't possibly let everybody go on sleeping in ignorance of such momentous news.

We approached the bell and looked at it with awe. It was a huge brass thing with a stout piece of rope hanging from the tongue, and it made the most *awful* noise when it rang. Even I found my spirit quailing a little at the thought of what we were about to do, but then we remembered the tidings of great joy we'd be bringing them and it seemed to us that anybody would forgive us in such circumstances.

I put out my hand, grasped the rope, and RANG! I rang and rang and rang and rang that bell. I thought: No good messing about. If we're going to do it, we'd better do it properly and make sure they *all* wake up.

They all woke up!

Hut doors flew open and bleary-eyed figures in pyjamas came stumbling out of them, asking what in the world was up.

I suppose it *was* rather a dirty trick to play on them: in wartime, alarm bells and sirens and other loud noises always meant something unpleasant was happening or would be happening soon.

Well, this time it was different. We shouted out the news to everyone, who in turn shouted it to the slow awakeners, and the shouts grew louder and louder all round the camp, and soon some of the officers began to appear, looking stern-faced and all ready to put everyone on a charge, until the news reached them too; whereupon we were immediately forgiven, and orders were issued to open up the Naafi and serve beer all round!

The Naafi staff reported that they hadn't got nearly enough beer to supply the whole camp; their stocks were low, etc, and immediately the Officers' Mess bar was opened and Naafi stocks were supplemented from there.

Everyone threw on battle-dress over their pyjamas and went whooping and prancing off to the Naafi, and an incredible orgy ensued, with beer flowing, tears flowing, Old Lang Syne echoing round the rafters, and everybody quite hysterical.

No one who has not lived through six years of killing and wounding, of long separations and of heartbreak, of forced work and withdrawal of all the kinds of freedom Englishmen have always taken for granted, can possibly understand what we felt in that hour; our overwhelming joy and relief and the sure knowledge that we'd soon be able to go home and take off our uniform and start to live a normal life – for most of us the first normal adult life we'd ever known.

We all got pretty drunk, but our eyes were glistening as we looked at each other and we realised that the long haul was over and that England was safe once more.

The party ended with the most colossal conga line you've ever seen; the entire camp joining together with hands on the waist in front, snaking out of the Naafi and into the first barrack hut and out the far end of that one and into the next one, and out of that one into the next one, and straight into the Officers' Mess (without so much as a by-your-leave) and round all their private little quarters and into their private little bedrooms and through their holy-of-holies, and out the far end of that and on and on through every building until we reached the Naafi again.

Then, around two in the morning, we all went yawning off, deliriously happy, to our beds and fell most soundly asleep.

And the poor old night watch which had relieved us missed it all, of course, and were very furious next morning!

10. SWEATING ON DEMOB

But of course it wasn't all beer and skittles after that, and we didn't all go home next day and live happily ever after.

To begin with, we had to wait another four months before V.J.Day (Victory in Japan). There was no question of any demobilisation until Britain ceased to be at war altogether.

Our feelings when we heard about Hiroshima were very mixed. First and foremost came feelings of colossal relief, that it was all really and truly over now, and there'd be no more killing. I don't think the enormity of it really hit us until a long time later. The utter horror was played down a bit, and few people realised the extent of the slaughter or the terrible nature of it. It was just relief, sheer relief, to everybody and it must also be remembered that we had no reason to feel anything but loathing of the Japanese.

After V.J.Day came and went, to my surprise and intense disappointment, nothing happened at all! We learned that demobilisation was going to be a long, slow process; comparable, in fact, with the process of mobilisation only in reverse, and it was then that I began to wish most fervently that I'd joined up a bit earlier. Everyone was given a demobilisation number, based on the length of time you'd been in, what family commitments you had, and how important your peacetime occupation was. So married men with families who had volunteered right at the beginning of the war were demobilised very quickly (and quite right too). And unmarried women without families who hadn't, like me, were right at the end of the queue!

I got terribly depressed. I'd had no idea it would be like that, though I suppose anyone with a grain of sense should have realised that the Powers That Be couldn't just wave goodbye to the entire army, navy and air force overnight and hurl them back into civilian life.

The actual machinery involved is mind-boggling: paying the gratuities, handing out demob suits, civilian ration books, clothing coupons – all the masses of red tape necessary to transform you from "One-oh-eight Miller" into a normal, unemployed young woman without a career, who knew very little about anything at all other than bashing a typewriter and twiddling the knobs on a radar set.

So, what happened was that we all went back on duty again as if nothing had happened. Aircraft still had to fly and to know where they were, and so did ships, including troopships bringing the boys home. All navigational aids would continue to be needed indefinitely (still are of course). So there was no slacking off for us.

But the thing had lost its kick. No blackboard in the ops room with the targets for the night chalked up on it. There weren't any targets. Thank God. But it did make a boring job even more boring. We all began to suffer from a strange new disease called "sweating on demob".

The numbers crept slowly up through the twenties, and to add to the misery of waiting for the thirties and then the forties, you began to lose your friends, some of whom had much lower numbers than you had; and goodbyes began to be part of the daily picture. Of course you all promised you'd keep in touch for evermore, but alas, you didn't and for most of us it was goodbye for keeps.

Few people live as closely together as members of the forces do, and for us it was not only the close proximity of our barrack huts but there was the watch system too, and with other members of your watch you ate your meals, spent hours on duty together and hours *off* duty too. So after many months of living in each other's pockets, you were suddenly shaking hands and hugging and kissing and wishing them all the best, and watching them go joyfully out of the camp for the last time, and into Civvy Street.

It was about this time that I began to feel distinctly peculiar. I would go up on duty, sit down at the set, and begin thinking about my home and family, and worrying about them and wondering what was happening to them. Completely illogical – what could be happening to them now? They weren't far away and I could ring them up if I wanted to. But the next thing I knew, I'd find myself in floods of tears! For no reason whatsoever! Nothing to cry about now (except boredom perhaps, and you don't cry with boredom).

I went on like this for a day or two, until the officer of the watch noticed me in tears on the set and asked me what was the matter. I couldn't tell him because I didn't know myself! He was very kind, and excused me the rest of the watch and told me to report sick in the morning. I didn't want to in the slightest. I thought, "How silly, to report sick when there's nothing to report!" But an order was an order and you had to carry it out, whatever your own feelings might be; so next morning found me on sick parade feeling a fine fool.

But I needn't have worried, because the moment the M.O. asked me what the trouble was I burst into tears again! I just couldn't stop this time, and the poor man must have wondered what on earth to do with me. In the end he decided that hysterical women weren't up his street at all, and he sent me off to the big bomber station at Bassingbourn, which had a large sick bay and plenty of medical staff and facilities.

I think I cried all the way there! I can remember being interrogated by another M.O. and finding nothing to say for myself beyond even more copious floods of tears, whereupon he gave me two tablets to swallow and I knew nothing at all for the next five hours or so.

I finally came to in a strange bed in a strange room, all alone, and very puzzled. A very kind nurse wearing the elegant uniform of Princess Mary's Nursing Service came in, and gave me a lovely meal of bacon and eggs and a pot of tea, and I began to feel half human again.

Presently the doctor came to see me. He asked a lot of questions about my career in the RAF to date, and a few rather nosy ones about my love life, then he gave me two more pills and out I went again like a light.

The following day I was told that I was suffering from "nervous exhaustion" and the MO started to try his hand at a bit of rather ham-fisted psychoanalysis. In fact he almost psychoanalysed himself into bed with me! I think he'd made up his mind that the whole trouble was that I was sex starved and that the best medicine for me would be himself!

What I wanted above everything else was to be allowed to go home. I formed a strong opinion that if I could only get home, even for a little while, I'd soon be as right as rain again. The trouble was that he wouldn't let me go home, because he had taken a fancy to me and wanted to apply his own therapeutic remedies to me.

I was allowed out during the day and I used to wander around the perimeter of the airfield chatting up the fitters who were working on the planes. I was definitely a bit unhinged, because I clearly remember having an overpowering desire to tell all of them all about it.

"I'm in the sick bay", I'd say. "There I was, sitting at my radar set one minute as right as rain and the next day I'd gone barmy! They sent me in here you see..."

The poor fitters looked at me with alarm and disappeared inside the cockpits. I just had this weird compulsion to tell everyone I met; it really was rather awful.

In the end, this rather frightful situation came to an end when the MO came to his senses and signed a certificate for six weeks' sick leave. Simply marvellous. Just what I wanted. I'd be home for Christmas!

My father was there when I arrived home, having already been demobbed (remember how nice and early *he* joined up) and he immediately set to work to try and make me better. He knew a bit about this sort of thing, having had a similar collapse himself once, and his therapy was, believe me, a whole lot better than that MO's! It involved a great deal of rest and a great deal of fresh air and exercise. There was also a doctor in Hoddesden who really *did* know his stuff.

At first I didn't want to go out at all, having reached

that stage where I wanted to crawl down a little hole and never mix with the outside world again.

But my father started me off with little walks of no more than a couple of hundred yards, with his arm on one side and a walking-stick on the other, because my legs felt all wobbly, especially going downhill. When we got home, I would feel as proud as if I'd run the marathon in the Olympics, and he would let me put my feet up and rest; and slowly I began to feel more human.

It all took time and patience. I remember the afternoon when he decided that I was well enough to try a visit to the cinema (probably Ginger Rogers was on and he was loath to miss her). I protested most vehemently and said I absolutely would not go. All those people, and all that noise! I just couldn't face it.

"Yes you can," he said. "And if you really do hate it, just say so and we'll leave at once."

This gave me sufficient courage to go in, and I did stay for the whole film. He was childishly pleased with himself and told everybody how well I was doing, which was just what I needed. Nobody poked fun at me, or told me to "pull myself together"; everyone was kind and understanding, but sufficiently firm to drag me back onto my feet again and force me to make the necessary effort.

Nervous breakdowns were not so common in those days, and it is a great credit to my family and the local doctor that I was given exactly the right treatment for speedy rehabilitation and a return to normal.

And so of course the inevitable day arrived when I had to return to Barkway, report for duty again, and wait for my demob number to come up. It was January 1946.

I was dreading it. Having had a taste of home life, how I longed to make it permanent! I think it was one of the hardest things I ever had to do, returning to camp and sweating on demob again.

But the Powers that Be had been doing a bit of thinking, apparently, and had come to the conclusion that I shouldn't return to duty on radar. I was to be assigned to the General Office. Somebody had found out that I was trained as a secretary! I'd tried so hard to keep away from office work, and I was going to have to finish up my wartime career bashing a typewriter!

I greeted the news with mixed feelings. I thought really that a change would be rather nice, and that it was partly the utter monotony of post-war radar that had sent me over the hill. But on the other hand – horror of horrors!" I would be a "NON-TECH"!! One of THEM! Not allowed in the Ops Block! Confined to the world of Admin (heavens!) and barred from my old stomping grounds.

Well, the hell with it, I thought. I'll just have to put up with it. And it's not as if there's anything secret going on in there any more, to feel shut out of. Why, even the Admin Officer was allowed in there now, for a good snoop around.

So I settled down to try to make something of my last spell of service life, pounding away at a very ancient Remington, and getting to bed at the same hour every night for the first time for many, many months.

I made those last few months in the Forces pass more quickly by learning to drive a car. There had been no chance of doing this of course. Private motoring and learning to drive had been virtually non-existent for six years. So I was thrilled when cycling around the roads near Barkway one day to see a sign outside a garage saying: LEARN TO DRIVE! – five shillings a lesson. I was really excited. Here at last was something enjoyable to do, which would stand me in good stead in civilian life, and in fact all my life.

He was a dear old boy, who gave me lessons in a dear old Austin Ten, and he always had a dear old drip on the end of his dear old reddish nose. We used to trundle around the almost deserted country roads around Royston, which was surely an ideal way of learning to drive, without being a menace to everyone else. I used to look foward to my lessons (which my father kindly paid for) and believe me, it was nice to have something to look forward to.

There was, of course, still the Blessed Day to look forward to, which began to come closer and closer. The discharge numbers at last crept into the forties, and my turn would be very soon. I typed away fairly happily all day long, and felt a hundred percent well. There was no sign of any recurrence of my nervous exhaustion, or whatever it was, nor has there ever been since. It was (thank God) just a one-off event, probably triggered by boredom and frustration, waiting to be freed, plus irregular sleep over a long period, and of course 'Nissen Hut Blues'!

And so at last in June 1946, more than a year after Germany surrendered and I'd rung that fire bell, my demob number was called and unbelievably I was the one shaking hands and kissing and hugging and getting my civilian ration book and my clothing coupons and my gratuity.

It was terribly exciting but at the same time scary. It would be like starting my life all over again. Learning how to be a grown-up really.

I was twenty-four, the world was at peace. I wouldn't

be having to take orders any more; no more uniform to wear; no more hair off the collar; no more biscuits; no more irons; no more jankers; no more nissen huts with everyone huddled round the stove; no more saluting; no more One-oh-Eight Miller!

But I'll tell you something. I wouldn't have missed a day of it! I don't envy anybody who didn't live through those stirring years. We may have grumbled and suffered a bit, but my goodness, we were *living*, you know. We were really living.

Ask any Waaf. Ask any Wren. Ask any AT.

Inside the Ops. Room at Barkway. This photo was taken after the war was over, and is very posed. Normally only the officer (standing, with telephone) would have been at the console. One operator would have been on the set (the apparatus with the clock on it) and no one but a mechanic would be touching the piece of apparatus on the right of the picture.

N.B. One-oh-Eight Miller seated at the console looks just about ready for that nervous breakdown!